Daily Breath Of

Prayers

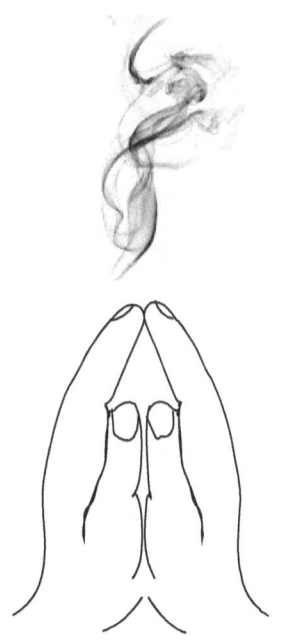

By: *Terry L. Ware, Sr.*

General Information

Daily Breath of Prayers

By: Terry L. Ware, Sr.

Cover Design: *Terry L. Ware, Sr.*

Published by: *B.O.S.S. Publishing*

Editor: *Terry L. Ware, Sr.*

ISBN: **978-0-9988341-6-0**

1. *Spiritual*   2. *Motivation*   3. *Inspiration*

First Edition

Dedication

This book is dedicated to those who are going through struggles in life and may feel they have lost themselves. For those that find it hard to find the words to say but are searching for change. For those that in spite of what they may be facing, choose to turn to God. May your hearts be filled with Gods Peace, Understanding, and comfort through these prayers…

Table of Contents

Daily Breath Of

Prayers

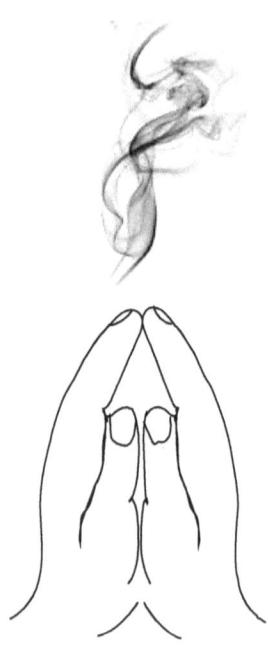

By: *Terry L. Ware, Sr.*

Introduction

Prayer is such a vital part of our lives which can and will help us through some of the most difficult challenges we may face in life. However, what does one do when they cannot find the words to say?

This book is a collection of prayers that myself and others have found that will give you the right words to say in some of the most trying times. As you go through these prayers, allow them to not only Bless, but help guide you with what to say as you pray to our Father in Heaven.

Prayer 1

Lead Me And I Will Follow

Heavenly Father, as You guide me on this journey, I will follow. Shape and mold my life that I may accomplish everything You need of me. In Jesus name, Amen.

_____

_____

_____

_____

_____

_____

_____

_____

_____

_____

_____

_____

_____

_____

_____

_____

_____

Prayer 2

Impart Within Me Your Peace

Gracious God, the storms of life can be overwhelming, but I choose to trust in You. To steadfastly focus on You! I ask that You fill and overwhelm me with Your peace. I love and trust You, In Jesus name, Amen.

_____

_____

_____

_____

_____

_____

_____

_____

_____

_____

_____

_____

_____

_____

_____

_____

Prayer 3

Your Love Is Pure

Heavenly Father, I am imperfect. I don't always say the right things. I sometimes jump to conclusions without first acknowledging You. My decisions aren't always right, and I don't know everything. But in the midst of my imperfections Your love for me never changes. You constantly look out for me, watching over me, keeping me safe in Your arms. I am truly grateful for the Love You have for me. In Jesus name, Amen.

_____

_____

_____

_____

_____

_____

_____

_____

_____

_____

_____

_____

_____

_____

_____

_____

_____

_____

Prayer 4

Give Me Your Sight

Gracious God, in the midst of feeling alone and frustrated, You are right there to give me a different perspective. What it looks like, is not the end! Thank you Father! In Jesus name, Amen.

_____

_____

_____

_____

_____

_____

_____

_____

_____

_____

_____

_____

_____

_____

_____

_____

_____

Prayer 5

You Are The Way

Heavenly Father, so many times I say, "my trust is in You", yet when faced with difficult situations I immediately try to find a way through. Thinking of things I can do to make it through and fail to acknowledge You. Lord, help my mind to be trained that as soon as difficulties hit, my mind will draw nigh unto You, and I immediately give it to You. In Jesus name, Amen.

_____

_____

_____

_____

_____

_____

_____

_____

_____

_____

_____

_____

_____

_____

_____

_____

_____

Prayer 6

Positive Outlook

Gracious God, my day will be based on my mindset that I begin with. So, I'll simply say, as You lead this day, I'll follow, which makes for one magnificent day! In Jesus name, Amen.

_____

_____

_____

_____

_____

_____

_____

_____

_____

_____

_____

_____

_____

_____

_____

_____

_____

_____

Prayer 7

Your Strength For Others

Heavenly Father, so many want to give up right now, for the hurt they feel runs deep. I pray now that You will not only comfort them, but give them Your Peace that eases their minds, that gives them a clearer view. Your word is true, for You will never leave them nor forsake them, but You'll always be right there with them to bring them through. In Jesus name, Amen.

Prayer 8

My Day Begins With You

Gracious God, I start my day acknowledging You, for You are my everything, and without You, I am nothing. In Jesus name, Amen.

Prayer 9

Leaving My Past Behind

Heavenly Father, my past is my past, thank You for forgiving me. Help me to forgive me and leave my past in the past, so that it will not get in the way of my present and future. In Jesus name, Amen.

_____

_____

_____

_____

_____

_____

_____

_____

_____

_____

_____

_____

_____

_____

_____

_____

_____

Prayer 10

Not My Will But Your Will

Gracious God, I digress, I can't figure it all out. As I trust in you more and more, give me a new outlook, a new vision, a new thought process, to never return to my own will. In Jesus name, Amen.

Prayer 11

Grateful In Spite of

Heavenly Father, my mind at times wonders "why"! But then I'm reminded, it has nothing to do with me, but everything to do with You! Despite my downfalls, Your love for me never changes. In Jesus name, Amen.

_____

_____

_____

_____

_____

_____

_____

_____

_____

_____

_____

_____

_____

_____

_____

_____

Prayer 12

Thankful

Gracious God, thank You! In Jesus name, Amen.

Prayer 13

I Get To Serve

Heavenly Father, I am a mess but I thank You for setting me apart. For giving me Your holiness within me to not only serve You, but to serve others for You. In Jesus name, Amen.

_____

_____

_____

_____

_____

_____

_____

_____

_____

_____

_____

_____

_____

_____

_____

_____

_____

_____

Prayer 14

It's Not About Me

Gracious God, thank You for the opportunities You have presented me with. Help me not to live a self-fulfilled life, but rather a life filled with helping others, doing Your will. In Jesus name, Amen.

_____

_____

_____

_____

_____

_____

_____

_____

_____

_____

_____

_____

_____

_____

_____

_____

Prayer 15

I Am Nothing Without You

Heavenly Father, where would I be without You? How could I cope with the things of life without You? How could I forgive without You? How could I breath without You? How could I love without You? I can do all things with You, but without You I would surely be lost. Thank You Father. In Jesus name, Amen.

_____

_____

_____

_____

_____

_____

_____

_____

_____

_____

_____

_____

_____

_____

_____

Prayer 16

I Choose To Believe You

Gracious God, It is not what it looks like, but rather what you have said. It Is So! In Jesus name, Amen.

_____

_____

_____

_____

_____

_____

_____

_____

_____

_____

_____

_____

_____

_____

_____

_____

_____

_____

Prayer 17

Today Will Be Different

Heavenly Father, as I am mindful of my thoughts today, I endeavor to be different than I was yesterday. My reactions of yesterday won't control my actions of today. In Jesus name, Amen.

<u>*Prayer 18*</u>

I Want To Love Like You

Gracious God, draw my heart closer and closer to You each day so that what comes out will be filled with Your Love. In Jesus name, Amen.

_____

_____

_____

_____

_____

_____

_____

_____

_____

_____

_____

_____

_____

_____

Prayer 19

I Need Your Wisdom And Strength

Heavenly Father, I don't have all the answers and most times I feel lost. Sometimes I find it hard to look up because of life's pains and struggles. Give me the strength to always look to You, even when my eyes are blinded to the answer that is You. In Jesus name, Amen.

Prayer 20

You Are My Source

Gracious God, it's so easy to get complacent and think I've arrived and began to take You for granted. No matter where You allow me to go, what You allow me to have, none of it will matter if I forget You're still my Source. I choose to never forget, but always look to You. In Jesus name, Amen.

_____

_____

_____

_____

_____

_____

_____

_____

_____

_____

_____

_____

_____

_____

_____

_____

Prayer 21

I Am Who You Say I Am

Heavenly Father, in this day and age it's so easy to look at what someone else has and want what they have or try to be like them. However, You created me to be me, one of a kind, unlike any other. Help me to learn more and more of me each day, so I'll never desire to be anyone else. In Jesus name, Amen.

Prayer 22

I Look Past My Fears

Gracious God, my desire is to do Your will and not my own. Help me to move past the fear that may come over me because of uncharted territory, in order to get to where I'm supposed to be. In Jesus name, Amen.

<u>*Prayer 23*</u>

My Desires Are Becoming My Needs

Heavenly Father, many times I get so caught up in what I desire, I never stop to ask You what I need. I yield to You Father; Your will be done in my life and not my own. In Jesus name, Amen.

Prayer 24

I Am Yours

Gracious God, fill me up until it's overflowing and others around me can not only see Your glory, but will be intrigued to know You for themselves. For You are more than enough. In Jesus name, Amen.

_____

_____

_____

_____

_____

_____

_____

_____

_____

_____

_____

_____

_____

_____

_____

Prayer 25

I Am Because You Are

Heavenly Father, because of You, I am more

than a conqueror. In Jesus name, Amen.

_____

_____

_____

_____

_____

_____

_____

_____

_____

_____

_____

_____

_____

_____

_____

_____

_____

Prayer 26

You Are Great

Gracious God, thank You for understanding me, even when I don't understand myself. Thank You for loving me, even in the times I fail to love myself. Thank You for always caring for me, even in the times I failed to care for myself. In Jesus name, Amen.

Prayer 27

Your Grace Is Sufficient

Heavenly Father, forgive me for trying to earn Your love rather than simply receiving Your love through grace. In Jesus name, Amen.

_____

_____

_____

_____

_____

_____

_____

_____

_____

_____

_____

_____

_____

_____

Prayer 28

Daily Covering

Gracious God, You have giving me another

day, I thank you for your grace. I pray for a covering

for my family and friends. May this day be a great

day for each of them. In Jesus name, Amen.

_____
_____
_____
_____
_____
_____
_____
_____
_____
_____
_____
_____
_____
_____
_____
_____
_____
_____

Prayer 29

Faith Before Anything

Heavenly Father, there is nothing too hard for You. Though I know this, at times my first reaction is doubt! Thank You for the obstacles that come to test my first reaction, in order to sharpen me towards making a better reaction, a Faith First reaction. In Jesus name, Amen.

Prayer 30

Being One In You

Gracious God, with everything that's going on in this world help me to show more Love towards others. It doesn't matter our skin color, for we are all created in Your image. In Jesus name, Amen.

Prayer 31

I Will Remain Focus

Heavenly Father, Thank You for the visions You have placed within me. Help me not to lose my focus when trying times come, but to continue to trust in You. In Jesus name, Amen.

_____

_____

_____

_____

_____

_____

_____

_____

_____

_____

_____

_____

_____

_____

_____

_____

_____

Prayer 32

I Am Not Alone

Gracious God, thank You for being with me every step of the way. Because of You, I can! In Jesus name, Amen.

_____

_____

_____

_____

_____

_____

_____

_____

_____

_____

_____

_____

_____

_____

_____

_____

_____

Prayer 33

Renew My Mind

Heavenly Father, if I continuously think the same, I will continuously do the same things. Renew my mind each day that I may continuously move forward daily. Help me to live in each new day with a new attitude. In Jesus name, Amen.

_____

_____

_____

_____

_____

_____

_____

_____

_____

_____

_____

_____

_____

_____

_____

_____

www.ingramcontent.com/pod-product-compliance
Lightning Source LLC
Chambersburg PA
CBHW051249180626
46816CB00004BA/1395